TIGGER COMES
TO THE FOREST

A. A. MILNE

Tigger Comes to the Forest

adapted by Stephen Krensky

with decorations by Ernest H. Shepard

Puffin Books

PUFFIN BOOKS
Published by the Penguin Group
Penguin Putnam Books for Young Readers, 345 Hudson Street, New York, New York 10014, U.S.A.
Penguin Books Ltd, 80 Strand, London WC2R ORL, England
Penguin Books Australia Ltd, Ringwood, Victoria, Australia
Penguin Books Canada Ltd, 10 Alcorn Avenue, Toronto, Ontario, Canada M4V 3B2
Penguin Books (N.Z.) Ltd, 182-190 Wairau Road, Auckland 10, New Zealand

Penguin Books Ltd, Registered Offices: Harmondsworth, Middlesex, England

First published in the United States of America by Dutton Children's Books and Puffin Books,
divisions of Penguin Putnam Books for Young Readers, 2002

3 5 7 9 10 8 6 4 2

This presentation, Copyright © 2002 by John Michael Brown, Peter Janson-Smith, Roger
Hugh Vaughan, Charles Morgan, and Timothy Michael Robinson, Trustees of the Pooh Properties
Winnie-the-Pooh, Copyright © 1926 by E. P. Dutton & Co., Inc.; Copyright renewal, 1954 by A. A. Milne
All rights reserved

Puffin Easy-to-Read ISBN 0-14-230185-X
Puffin® and Easy-to-Read® are registered trademarks of Penguin Putnam Inc.

Printed in China

Reading Level 2.2

CONTENTS

1

TIGGER MAKES AN APPEARANCE

Winnie-the-Pooh woke up suddenly

in the night and listened.

Then he got out of bed and lit his candle.

He stumped across the room

to see if anyone was trying

to get into his honey-cupboard.

They weren't, so he stumped back again

and got into bed.

Then he heard the noise again.

"Is that you, Piglet?" he said.

But it wasn't.

"Come in, Christopher Robin."

But Christopher Robin didn't.

"Worraworraworraworraworra,"

said Whatever-it-was.

"What can it be?" thought Pooh.

"It isn't a growl,

and it isn't a purr,

and it isn't a bark.

It's a noise made by a strange animal.

And he's making it outside my door.

So I shall get up

and ask him not to do it."

Pooh got out of bed

and opened his front door.

"Hallo!" said Pooh.

"Hallo!" said Whatever-it-was.

"Who is it?" said Pooh.

"Me," said a voice.

"Oh!" said Pooh.

"Well, come here. I'm Pooh."

"I'm Tigger," said Tigger.

"Oh!" said Pooh.

"Does Christopher Robin

know about you?"

"Of course he does," said Tigger.

"Well," said Pooh,

"it's the middle of the night,

which is a good time

for going to sleep.

Tomorrow morning we'll have

some honey for breakfast.

Do Tiggers like honey?"

"They like everything," said Tigger.

"If they like going to sleep

on the floor," said Pooh,

"I'll go back to bed.

Good night."

When he awoke in the morning,

the first thing he saw was Tigger

looking at himself in the mirror.

"Hallo!" said Pooh.

"Hallo!" said Tigger.

"I've found somebody just like me."

Pooh got out of bed,

and began to explain

what a mirror was.

"Excuse me a moment," said Tigger.

"There's something climbing up your table."

With one loud

Worraworraworraworraworra

he jumped at the end of the tablecloth,

pulled it to the ground,

and wrapped himself up in it three times.

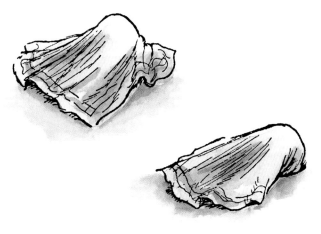

After a terrible struggle,

he got his head into the daylight again.

"Have I won?" he said cheerfully.

"That's my tablecloth," said Pooh,

as he began to unwind Tigger.

"I wondered what it was," said Tigger.

Pooh put the cloth back on the table.

Then he put a large honey-pot

on the cloth,

and they sat down to breakfast.

Tigger took a large mouthful of honey,

and then looked up at the ceiling.

He made exploring noises

and considering noises

and what-have-we-got-*here* noises.

Then he said in a very decided voice:

"Tiggers don't like honey."

"Oh!" said Pooh.

"I thought they liked everything."

"Everything except honey," said Tigger.

Pooh said that as soon as

he had finished,

he would take Tigger

to Piglet's house.

There Tigger could try

some of Piglet's haycorns.

"Thank you, Pooh," said Tigger.

"Haycorns is really

what Tiggers like best."

2

TIGGER MEETS A VERY SMALL ANIMAL

So after breakfast

Pooh and Tigger went round

to see Piglet.

Pooh explained as they went

that Piglet was a Very Small Animal

who didn't like bouncing.

So Pooh asked Tigger

not to be too Bouncy at first.

Tigger, who had been hiding

behind trees

and jumping out on Pooh's shadow,

said that Tiggers were only bouncy

before breakfast.

So by and by they knocked

at the door of Piglet's house.

"Hallo, Pooh," said Piglet.

"Hallo, Piglet. This is Tigger."

"Oh, is it?" said Piglet.

He edged round to the other side

of the table.

"I thought Tiggers

were smaller than that."

"Not the big ones," said Tigger.

"They like haycorns," said Pooh.

"And poor Tigger

hasn't had any breakfast."

Piglet pushed the bowl of haycorns

towards Tigger.

"Help yourself," he said.

Tigger filled his mouth with haycorns.

After a long munching noise, he said:

"Ee-ers o i a-ors."

"What?" said Pooh and Piglet.

"Skoos ee," said Tigger,

and went outside for a moment.

When he came back, he said firmly:

"Tiggers don't like haycorns."

"You said

they liked everything

except honey," said Pooh.

"Everything except honey

and haycorns,"

explained Tigger.

"Oh, I see!" said Pooh.

"What about thistles?" asked Piglet.

"Thistles," said Tigger,

"is what Tiggers like best."

"Then let's go along and see Eeyore,"

said Piglet.

So the three of them went.

3

TIGGER TRIES TO EAT A THISTLE

After they had walked and walked,

they came to the part of the Forest

where Eeyore was.

"Hallo, Eeyore!" said Pooh.

"This is Tigger."

Eeyore walked all round Tigger one way.

Then he turned and walked

all round him the other way.

"What did you say it was?" he asked.

"Tigger."

"Ah!" said Eeyore.

"He's just come," explained Piglet.

"Ah!" said Eeyore again.

He thought for a long time and then said:

"When is he going?"

Pooh explained that Tigger
was a great friend of Christopher Robin's,
who had come to stay in the Forest.

"And Tiggers always eat thistles.

That was why we came to see you, Eeyore."

Eeyore led the way

to the most thistly-looking patch of thistles

that ever was.

"A little patch I was keeping

for my birthday," he said.

"But, after all, what are birthdays?

Here today and gone tomorrow.

Help yourself, Tigger."

Tigger thanked him

and looked a little anxiously at Pooh.

"Are these really thistles?" he whispered.

"Yes," said Pooh.

"What Tiggers like best?"

"That's right," said Pooh.

"I see," said Tigger.

So he took a large mouthful,

and he gave a large crunch.

"Ow!" he said.

He sat down and put his paw

in his mouth.

"What's the matter?" asked Pooh.

"Hot!" mumbled Tigger,

shaking his head

to get the prickles out.

"Tiggers don't like thistles."

"But you said," began Pooh,

"that Tiggers like everything

except honey and haycorns."

"*And* thistles," said Tigger.

Pooh looked at him sadly.

"What are we going to do?"

he asked Piglet.

Piglet knew the answer to that.

They must go and see

Christopher Robin.

"You'll find him with Kanga,"

said Eeyore.

Pooh nodded and called to Tigger.

"We'll go and see Kanga.

She's sure to have

lots of breakfast for you."

"Come on!" Tigger said,

and he rushed off.

4

TIGGER FINALLY EATS BREAKFAST

Pooh and Piglet walked slowly after Tigger.

And as they walked

Piglet said nothing,

because he couldn't think of anything.

And Pooh said nothing,

because he was thinking of a poem.

And when he had thought of it,

he began:

What shall we do about

poor little Tigger?

If he never eats nothing, he'll

never get bigger.

He doesn't like honey and haycorns

and thistles

Because of the taste and because of

the bristles.

And all the good things which an

animal likes

Have the wrong sort of swallow or

too many spikes.

Tigger had been bouncing

in front of them all this time,

turning round every now and then

to ask, "Is this the way?"

Now at last they came to

Kanga's house,

and there was Christopher Robin.

Tigger rushed up to him.

"Oh, there you are, Tigger!"

said Christopher Robin.

"I knew you'd be somewhere."

"I've been finding things in the Forest,"

said Tigger importantly.

"I've found a pooh and a piglet

and an eeyore.

But I can't find any breakfast."

Pooh and Piglet explained

what had been happening.

"Don't *you* know what Tiggers like?"

asked Pooh.

"I expect if I thought very hard I should,"

said Christopher Robin.

"But I *thought* Tigger knew."

"I do," said Tigger.

"Everything there is in the world

except honey and haycorns and—

what were those hot things called?"

"Thistles."

"Yes, and those."

"Oh, well then," said Christopher Robin,

"Kanga can give you some breakfast."

So they went into Kanga's house.

And Roo said, "Hallo, Pooh,"

and "Hallo, Piglet" once,

and "Hallo, Tigger" twice,

because he had never said it before

and it sounded funny.

Then they told Kanga what they wanted.

"Well, look in my cupboard, Tigger dear,"

Kanga said very kindly,

"and see what you'd like."

But the more Tigger put his nose

into this and his paw into that,

the more things he found

which Tiggers didn't like.

"What happens now?" he said

when he had tried everything

in the cupboard.

Kanga, Christopher Robin, and Piglet

were all standing round Roo,

watching him have his Extract of Malt.

"Must I?" said Roo.

"Now, Roo dear," said Kanga,

"you remember what you promised."

"What is it?" whispered Tigger to Piglet.

"His Strengthening Medicine," said Piglet.

"He hates it."

So Tigger came closer, and he leaned over

the back of Roo's chair.

Suddenly he put out his tongue,

and took one large golollop.

"Oh!" said Kanga,

pulling the spoon out of Tigger's mouth.

But the Extract of Malt was gone.

"Tigger *dear!*" said Kanga.

"He's taken my medicine,"

sang Roo happily.

"He's taken my medicine!

He's taken my medicine!"

Then Tigger looked up at the ceiling.

He closed his eyes,

and his tongue went round and round.

A peaceful smile came over his face.

"So *that's* what Tiggers like!" he said.

Which explains why he always lived

at Kanga's house afterwards.

Tigger had Extract of Malt

for breakfast, dinner, and tea.

And sometimes, when Kanga thought

Tigger wanted strengthening,

he had a spoonful or two

of Roo's breakfast as medicine.

"But *I* think," said Piglet to Pooh,

"that he's been strengthened

quite enough."